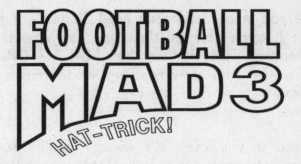

FOOTBALL MAD 3
HAT-TRICK!

"Oi, Thompson!" Mr Carlton bellowed. "Was that you?"

"Sorry, sir," said Danny. "I..."

Mr Carlton strode towards him. "Just keep on the way you're going," he said, "and you're out. All right?" He paused. "And I thought I told you to smarten up your appearance a bit. Hair flopping around all over your face. How do you expect to play when you can't even see the ball properly?" His face twisted up with contempt. "You look like a big girl."

If you enjoyed **Football Mad 3,** find out how St Botolph's bagged their first two trophies in **Football Mad,** and **Football Mad 2 – Offside!** also by Paul Stewart. They're *storming* good reads!

And if you can't get enough quality soccer writing, check out Haydn Middleton's hilarious FA Cup-based mini-series:

1. Come and Have a Go if You Think You're SMART Enough!
2. Come and Have a Go if You Think You're COOL Enough!
3. Come and Have a Go if You Think You're MAD Enough!
4. Come and Have a Go if You Think You're RICH Enough!

Or why not try Rob Childs' cracking soccer adventures across space and time – join the **Time Rangers** for:

1. **A Shot in the Dark**
2. **A Blast From the Past**
3. **A Race Against Time**
4. **A Ghost of a Chance**
5. **A Toss of the Coin**
6. **A Sting in the Tale**
7. **A Time for a Change**
8. **A Fate Worse Than Death**
9. **A Band on the Run**

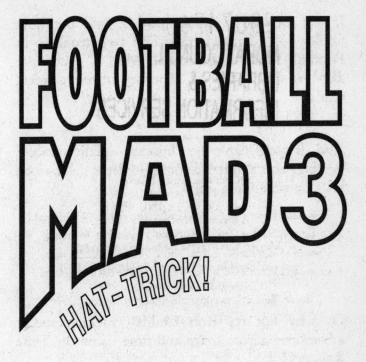

FOOTBALL MAD 3

HAT-TRICK!

Paul Stewart

Hippo

Scholastic Children's Books,
Commonwealth House,
1-19 New Oxford Street,
London WC1A 1NU, UK
A division of Scholastic Ltd
London ~ New York ~ Toronto ~ Sydney ~ Auckland
Mexico City ~ New Delhi ~ Hong Kong

First published in the UK by Scholastic Ltd, 1999

Copyright © Paul Stewart, 1999
Inside illustrations copyright © David Kearney, 1999

ISBN 0 439 01114 0

Typeset by
Cambrian Typesetters, Frimley, Camberley, Surrey
Printed by
Cox & Wyman Ltd, Reading, Berks

2 4 6 8 10 9 7 5 3

for Joseph, Michael
and Phillip

Chapter 1

"Oi, Thompson!" screamed a voice from the touchline.

Danny froze. It was Mr Carlton, sports teacher and team coach, doing the shouting. Surely he wasn't about to suggest that Danny could have got to the ball? It was *miles* away! Then again, Danny thought miserably, the man was always picking on him. He turned round slowly to be confronted by Mr Carlton's angry face glaring back at him.

"Who do you think you are, Thompson?" he bellowed. "Bloomin' Cinderella?"

"Sir?" said Danny, reddening with embarrassment.

"You keep running away from the ball, lad!" he said.

A titter of amusement ran round the opposing team.

At the other end of the pitch, Gary Connell groaned. As captain, it was his job to keep spirits high. At 1–0 down, however, and with only ten minutes of the match remaining, morale was already low among the players of the St Botolph's team. And having their own coach taking the mickey was not helping matters.

"Come on then, you lot," Gary shouted encouragingly. "It's not over yet!"

"It soon will be," jeered his opposite number.

Gary ignored the comment. Yet, as he called out to Craig to pass him the ball, there was a hint of desperation in his voice. "Now!" he yelled as he sped up the centre of the pitch. "NOW!"

Craig floated the ball up towards him. Gary trapped it easily as it struck the ground. The next moment three defenders raced in all at once, seized it from him and punted it back up into the St Botolph's half.

Gary cursed under his breath as yet another opportunity to score was snuffed out. If they were to stand any chance of winning the Mereside Borough Junior Cup, then they had to draw with Holmbury at the very least. But that equalizing goal was proving elusive – and the last precious minutes were ticking away.

As Juniors, Gary, Danny, Craig and the rest had won the cup for two years in succession. Now, as under-twelve Seniors, it was the last time they would be able to enter the tournament. The competition had, as always, been hard fought all season. St Botolph's were currently sharing the lead position in their group. If they did manage to go through to the final – and win! – then the cup would become theirs to keep.

The trouble was, every team they played seemed determined that this should not happen. Even Holmbury – a bunch of no-hopers who stood no chance of winning the cup – were playing the game of their lives in an attempt to prevent St Botolph's achieving that all-important hat-trick. Having scored a lucky goal in the twenty-fourth minute they were holding on to their lead tenaciously. No matter what St Botolph's tried, the Holmbury players were always there to close down every move, every set-piece, every charge at goal.

Gary glanced at his watch. Even with time for stoppages added on, there were barely five minutes to go. Victory was certainly out of the question, and the draw they so desperately needed was looking less and less likely – when suddenly, all that changed.

"Foul!" Luke Edwards appealed, as the Holmbury number five sent Maurice Meacham flying.

The referee hesitated for a moment. Gary held his breath. Would he or wouldn't he award them a free kick?

The whistle blew. "Yes!" Gary cried.

He strode up the pitch towards the waiting ball, all too aware that this was likely to be their last chance to save the match. He nodded grimly at Craig. It was time to try out one of the set-pieces they'd been practising.

"Ten metres!" the ref was shouting at the defenders, who were standing in a wall in front of the ball. Reluctantly, they shuffled back a little. "TEN metres, I said!" the ref insisted.

Finally satisfied, he waved play on. Craig and Gary stepped away from the ball. Then, Craig ran up, drew back his foot – and jumped to the left. As he did so, Gary rushed forwards and booted the ball hard.

The kick was a beaut. It soared past the players in the wall and over to the right-hand side of the field in a low dipping arc, where Luke was already racing up the field to meet it. With all the defenders so far forwards, he was soon past them.

"Offside!" the Holmbury team and supporters shouted out in unison. "OFFSIDE!"

But the assistant's flag remained down. The set-piece had worked to perfection. When Luke had started his run, as the ball was struck, there had been half a dozen defenders between him and the goal. It was very much *on*side. Now, all he

had to do was complete the move by scoring!

"Come on, Luke!" Gary bellowed, as Luke gathered the ball neatly and flicked it forwards.

The St Botolph's supporters began cheering.

"Go on, Luke! You can do it!"

Still stinging from Mr Carlton's remarks, Danny bit into his lower lip and watched grimly as Holmbury's goalie raced out of his area towards the attacker. Although he was playing in defence, Danny was a natural goalkeeper. He had always played in goal for the juniors and it was only because Mr Carlton had insisted that Ricky Baker be put in in his place that he was not there now.

He knew that rushing the attacker was the goalie's only option. To close the angle. To force a mistake. Or, if he was fast – and brave – enough, to seize the ball before a shot could be taken. Danny's heart was racing. His head pounded.

"Come on, Luke!" he muttered. "Take it easy and..."

At that moment, Luke nudged the ball on to his left foot and booted it with everything he had. The ball rose. A hush fell.

The goalie leapt up in a desperate flying attempt to deflect the ball, but it whistled past his outstretched fingers untouched. On and on the ball went, curving in as it flew. The St Botolph's team held their breath as one. Would the shot find the goal, or was it doomed to speed past the far post for a goalkick – and certain defeat?

The next moment, their question was answered.

"YEAH!" roared the St Botolph's supporters as the ball clipped the inside of the post and span back into the corner of the net.

"YEAH!" cried the St Botolph's team.

Luke fell to his knees and clasped his hands together as the rest of the team clustered round to congratulate him.

"Brilliant, Luke, mate!" Gary said.

"Fantastic goal!" said Craig.

"Amazing!" "Tremendous!" "Ace!" The compliments came thick and fast.

Holmbury kicked off again, but the ball hadn't even left the centre-circle when the ref blew the final whistle. As the teams made their way back to the changing rooms, St Botolph's were jubilant. They'd managed to get that all-important draw. Of course, winning the cup was still by no means a certainty, but they were still in with a chance – and that was what counted.

Chapter 2

Only one person was less than delighted with the result, and that was Mr Carlton. Short and stocky, with thick black hair and dark eyes, he paced the St Botolph's changing room like a caged bear.

"Call yourself a football team," he complained, his nasal voice more whiny than ever. "You played like a load of old women!" Their mood instantly punctured, the boys sat round on the bench, staring miserably down at the floor. "A draw! Against that shower! It could have been – it *should* have been – 5–0. At least."

Gary looked up. "Yeah, but we are still in with a chance, sir," he said. "If we beat Mickelham Mill in the next match, and if Eastfields lose against Milton, and then if..."

"Pfff," said Mr Carlton dismissively, cutting him short. "Sounds like an awful lot of *ifs* to me." He looked round at the lowered heads. "You know what?" he said at length. "I don't think you lot are up to it. You've got no discipline. You're ragged..." He turned and fixed his gaze on Danny. "And as for you, Thompson!" he said.

Danny's heart sank. It was happening again. Whatever the situation, it was always him who bore the brunt of Mr Carlton's anger and contempt. He continued to stare down at the floor with his hair over his eyes; head thumping, cheeks ablaze.

"Sloppy *and* slow. You excelled yourself," he added scornfully. "Are you listening to me, lad?"

Danny looked up wearily. "Yes, sir," he said. "I did my best. I—"

"Yeah, well, that's the problem, isn't it?" Mr Carlton said. "Your best just isn't good enough. In fact, maybe it's time we thought about whether there's room for you in the team at all."

Danny gasped. Room in the team? But he'd *always* played in the team! All round him he could feel the eyes of his team-mates staring at him – team-mates, he knew, who were only too relieved that Mr Carlton was picking on him rather than on them. His face burned with the unfairness of it all. His eyes watered. There was a lump in his throat that wouldn't be swallowed away.

"And don't start blubbing on me," Mr Carlton said furiously. "If you improve – your game, your attitude, your appearance – then maybe I'll keep you on. If not..."

The loaded words hung in the air as Mr Carlton strode across the changing room. At the door he paused, turned back and glared at Danny. His brow furrowed. "It's up to you, lad," he said darkly. "It's all up to you."

Danny nodded weakly. He didn't feel it was up to him at all. Football had always been the greatest love in his life. He, Craig and Gary had played up the rec together for as far back as any of them could remember and, from the time they'd started school, they'd played in the same team together. Yet ever since they'd moved up from the Juniors to the Seniors, everything had gone wrong.

Unlike Mr Talbot, who coached the junior school team, Mr Carlton was a harsh man, a hard man – a man who, from the first time they'd met, had taken an instant dislike to Danny Thompson. And for his part, Danny did not have a clue why.

The worst of it was, Mr Carlton was right about Danny's need to improve. The constant teasing and taunting and goading had had its effect on the boy. He'd lost his confidence both on and off the pitch. At the time it had happened, Danny felt that being taken out of goal and put into defence was the last straw. He didn't think things could get any worse. Now, with the threat of being dropped from the team hanging over his head, he realized that they certainly could.

As Mr Carlton slammed the door shut behind him, the whole team breathed a sigh of relief. Gary climbed to his feet, crossed the room and patted his friend on the back.

"It'll be all right, mate," he said. "You'll see."

A ripple of agreement went round.

"I'll talk to him," Gary promised. "As captain. See if I can't get you back in goal where you belong." He turned to Ricky. "You won't mind that, will you?"

Ricky Baker shook his head. "Course not," he said. "Danny's a far better goalie than I'll ever be." He laughed. "Damn him!"

Danny smiled. He appreciated the support from the rest of the team, and he knew that Gary would do his best for him. In the end, though, there was nothing any of them could do if Mr Carlton did decide to drop him.

Later that evening, Gary, Craig and Danny met up the rec for a kick around – something they had been doing for as far back as any of them could remember. The previous year, Leigh Parker – a new boy – had often joined them. But Leigh's family had moved on once more, and the boys were back to being a threesome again.

Floodlights had recently been put in around the new clay pitch at the far end of the park, which meant that they could continue their game even when it got dark – not that any of them felt much like playing that particular evening. Their hearts were simply not in it.

It was seven o'clock when Danny announced that he'd had enough. "I'm off home," he said simply as, head down, he set off towards the park gates.

Gary picked up the ball. "Hang on, then," he said. "We'll come with you."

Danny kept walking. "I just want to be on my own," he said.

Gary looked at Craig and shrugged.

"Come on, Danny," Craig called out. "It's gonna be fine. He can't drop you from the team. We won't let him."

Danny stopped, spun round and looked up. His eyes were wet with tears. "Oh yeah?" he said. "And what can you do to stop him?"

"I told you," Gary said. "I'm gonna talk to him."

"We all will," said Craig, nodding enthusiastically. "At Friday's training session."

"There's several things I want to bring up," said Gary. "For a start, we've got to sort out this stupid Christmas tree he's got us playing in..."

"Too right," Craig agreed. "It puts far too much pressure on the wide players." He grinned. "And *I* should know."

Although popular for a while, the so-called Christmas tree formation of 3–5–2 had been largely discredited at both amateur and professional levels. The main problem with it was that the wingers were expected to cover the whole of their line, including defence. All too often, it led to dangerous gaps opening up at the back during an opposition attack.

"We need to play a more solid 4–4–2," said Gary.

"Or even 4–2–4," said Craig. "It's more attacking. We've got to win the next two matches, don't forget."

"Whatever," said Gary. "And I'll bring up the goalie thing at the same time." He smiled at Danny. "Like I said I would."

Danny hung his head. "It won't do any good," he said.

"Come on, Danny. It's not—" Craig began.

"Not what?" Danny interrupted sharply. "Not that bad? Not the end of the world? It is to me." He looked back and forwards between his two friends. "What's the matter with him anyway?" he said. "What's he got against me? What have I ever done to him?"

Craig and Gary shuffled about awkwardly. It was Craig who spoke first.

"It's not you," he said slowly. "Do you remember back in Year Five? Miss MacDonald. The way she was always picking on Judy Reeves?"

"Yeah," said Danny. "So what?"

"Well, it's the same, isn't it?" said Craig. "Underneath the strictness, teachers like her and Mr Carlton are weak. They're frightened of losing control – so they have to find a scapegoat..."

"Yeah, you're right," said Gary admiringly – he hadn't realized that Craig was such a good judge of character. He turned back to Danny.

"No one likes Mr Carlton, so he picks on you to try and win the rest of us round." He snorted. "I tell you what, though. It isn't working."

"Isn't it?" said Danny glumly. "What if the others think I ought to be dropped?"

"But they don't," Gary and Craig replied in unison.

"Yeah, but..."

"Danny," said Craig. "All they're interested in is getting the best team together to win the cup for the third time. The hat-trick. And you're the best goalie we've got."

Danny clenched his teeth and struggled hard to fight back the tears. "I wish Mr Berryman could take over the football team," he said. "*He* never picks on me!"

The others nodded glumly. Mr Berryman was a student teacher who had taken the occasional PE lesson as part of his training. He was young and smiley; his lessons were fun – and everybody liked him.

Gary shrugged. "I think we're going to be lumbered with Mr Carlton for a long time yet," he said.

"I know," said Danny angrily. "And I hate him. I really really hate him. The rotten, stinking, loud-mouthed..." He turned away. "If only there was something I could do to get back at him."

Gary smiled. "I'm sure we can think of something," he said. "But let's see what happens on Friday first, before we make any plans. All right?"

Danny nodded. "All right," he said.

Chapter 3

In the event, the training session that Friday couldn't have been worse. The moment they emerged on to the pitch, it was clear that Mr Carlton was not a happy man. He snapped at them for being late. He shouted at Maurice and Luke for talking. And when Gary attempted to talk to him about dropping the Christmas tree formation for a more conventional line-up, he turned on the boy with white-faced fury.

"I will not have you challenging my authority, Connell," he raged. "Do you understand me?"

"Sir," Gary mumbled.

"I hope you do, lad." He snorted. "If you value being captain, that is." He turned away and blew his whistle. "Right, once round the field, all of you. Then back here for twenty press-ups, twenty sit-ups and twenty burpees. Go!"

The boys sprinted away. None of them particularly enjoyed warming up, but today it was a relief just to get away from Mr Carlton and his foul temper. They hoped his mood might have improved by the time they got back. They hoped in vain.

"Keep your backs straight," he yelled when they were doing their press-ups. "Count to *five* on every sit-up," he shouted a few minutes later. "And put some effort into it!" he bellowed as they got to the burpees. "Squat-thrust, star-jump! Squat-thrust, star-jump! Come on, Connell, stop slacking!"

Gary caught Danny's eye and grimaced. Danny shrugged.

"Now you know what it's like," he whispered.

"Oi, Thompson!" Mr Carlton bellowed. "Was that you?"

"Sorry, sir," said Danny. "I..."

Mr Carlton strode towards him. "Just keep on the way you're going," he said, "and you're out. All right?" He paused. "And I thought I told you to smarten up your appearance a bit. Hair flopping around all over your face. How do you expect to play when you can't even see the ball properly?" His face twisted up with contempt. "You look like a big girl."

Somebody sniggered.

Danny blushed and shrivelled up inside. "I... I..." he faltered. He'd been so intent on playing well that he'd forgotten all about Mr Carlton's criticism of his attitude and appearance. "Sorry, sir. Mum said I could get a haircut at the weekend," he lied. "If that's all right."

"If that's what *Mummy* said, I suppose it'll have to be," Mr Carlton replied sarcastically.

For a second time, somebody sniggered. Gary looked round angrily to see who it was. Mr Carlton, on the other hand, took it as confirmation that the rest of the team were with him on this.

"A mummy's boy or a big girl?" he said. "Which one are you then, Thompson? Eh?"

Danny bit into his lower lip. "N–neither, sir," he said quietly.

Mr Carlton sneered. "Then prove it," he said. "Show me what you're really made of. Impress me."

"Sir," said Danny, as he threw himself back into the exercises.

Mr Carlton finally turned away.

"Right then," he announced. "Get yourselves into pairs. One at each end of the lines of cones. And I want to see you controlling those balls as if they were stuck to your boots, all right?" He raised his whistle and blew. "Go."

Gary teamed up with Danny. When the whistle sounded, he dribbled the ball expertly in and out of the cones towards him. "Good luck," he muttered as he passed the ball.

Danny nodded but said nothing. He knew it would take more than luck to impress Mr Carlton. He'd need to play with skill, with speed, with accuracy – he'd need to play twice as well as anyone else if Mr Carlton wasn't to start picking on him again. And given the state of his trembling legs and churning stomach, that wasn't going to be easy.

At the third cone, Danny stumbled awkwardly. The ball slipped away out of control, and when he tried to retrieve it he over-reached himself, caught his heel on the top of the ball, and fell heavily to the ground.

Mr Carlton laughed unpleasantly "Forget your stick, did you?" he said.

"S—sorry, sir," Danny mumbled.

He climbed shakily to his feet and struggled bravely to carry on, but it was hopeless. His dribbling got no better, and his tackling, heading and passing were all worse. The trouble was, Danny was nervous. The harder he tried, the stiffer he moved. The stiffer he moved, the more mistakes he made. And the more mistakes he made, the more nervous he became. The whole training session was turning into a nightmare.

Mr Carlton blew his whistle. "Right then, lads," he said. "A five minute break, then we'll have a match for the last half-hour. Six-a-side. I'll stop the game every time something crops up that I think you can learn from. All right?"

The boys nodded happily. It was unlike Mr Carlton to have such a relaxed ending to a session. Only Danny remained uneasy and with good reason, for, from the moment the game started it was instantly clear to him what was happening.

His first header was greeted with a sharp blow on the whistle. "Stop! Stop!" Mr Carlton yelled. "Where the hell was that header meant to be aimed, Thompson? Good grief, lad, you've got a head like a sheriff's badge."

A snigger went round the team. Even Gary found it hard not to grin. Mr Carlton looked round, a smile tugging at the corners of his tight mouth.

"Point one," he said. "If you can't head the ball, take it on the chest and let it drop to your feet."

He blew the whistle to start the match again. And stopped it a moment later with a furious whistle-blast.

"Thompson has just committed the cardinal sin," he said. "Who can tell me what it was?"

"He passed the ball across his own penalty area, sir," said Maurice Meacham smugly.

"He passed the ball across his own penalty area," Mr Carlton repeated. He turned on Danny. "You never, *ever* pass the ball across your own penalty area. Got that? Good grief, lad, this is so basic!"

Danny nodded miserably and turned away. The game re-started. The interruptions continued. Every time Danny tried something it led to the whistle being blown again – yet when he held back, the same thing happened.

"Stick with your man," Mr Carlton bellowed. "Go in hard!"

Danny was at a loss to know what to do. Even his throw-in led to the whistle being blown.

"That," said Mr Carlton triumphantly to the others, "was a foul throw. Did you see the ball spinning? Which means Thompson has given away possession. And what is it I'm always telling you? Connell?"

Gary swallowed. He didn't want to get his friend into even more trouble – but then again, neither did he want to give Mr Carlton an excuse to take the captain's job away from him.

"You can't score if you haven't got the ball," he muttered.

"What was that?" Mr Carlton said, his hand raised theatrically to his ear.

Gary repeated himself, louder this time.

"Pre-*cise*-ly!" Mr Carlton crowed. "You can't score if you haven't got the ball – and if that's not clear, then you may as well give up." He checked his watch. "Right. It's half-past four," he said. "Go and get showered."

As one, the boys turned and headed for the changing room. Nobody ran. Nobody spoke. Danny, for his part, felt worse than he'd ever felt in his life. He'd been humiliated in front of his team-mates and his friends – not once, but time after time after time. He'd been used to point out each and every mistake in their game. Who could blame them now if they didn't want him in the team?

"Thompson. Come here, lad."

Now what? thought Danny un-happily. For a moment, he was tempted to ignore the man. To keep on walking and never come back. But then, he thought, wouldn't that just be giving in? He stopped and looked round.

"I said, here," said Mr Carlton quietly.

Danny hesitated. He didn't seem so angry now. Maybe he wasn't going to have another go at him after all. He walked across the grass towards the teacher.

Mr Carlton placed his hands on his hips. "That really wasn't very good, was it?" he said.

Danny looked down. "No, sir," he said.

"I said I wanted to see an improvement in your appearance, your attitude and your game." He breathed in. "I didn't see evidence of any of those."

Danny swallowed and began chewing the skin on the inside of his cheek. He wanted to cry. He wanted to scream. He wanted the ground to swallow him up.

Mr Carlton bent down towards him. "If you don't want to be in the team, why don't you just say?" he said. "Playing like that..."

Danny's head jerked upwards. "But I do want to be in the team," he blurted out. "It's just... You make... I get..." He turned away.

He wanted to tell Mr Carlton that it was all his fault. That he frightened him. And that the more frightened he became the worse he played. But how could you tell a teacher something like that? *How?*

"Well?" Mr Carlton demanded.

Danny shook his head. "Nothing, sir," he said.

"Nothing," Mr Carlton repeated flatly. "Which is exactly what you've contributed to this training session. Big fat nothing. And I won't have it! You'll do four laps of the field before you go and shower."

"But, sir," Danny began.

"NOW!" Mr Carlton roared.

Fighting back the tears, Danny spun round and ran off, out across the grass,

towards the perimeter fence and away from the horrible man who seemed hellbent on making his life a misery.

On and on, he ran. As he rounded the far posts he noticed Mr Carlton disappearing inside the changing rooms, and cursed the man under his breath. And when that didn't make him feel any better, he raised his head and bellowed as loud as he could. The angry words were whipped away on the wind.

Shouting, Danny realized, was pointless. He needed to *do* something. But what?

A fine drizzle had begun to fall and, as Danny went into his second lap, it cooled his burning cheeks and helped him think more clearly. He realized that what he wanted was to give Mr Carlton a dose of his own medicine. To humiliate him in front of the others, just as Mr Carlton had done to him so many times. To make him feel stupid. Awkward. Embarrassed.

Round and round, he went, past the far posts for a third time and back round to the start. The rain grew heavier.

Certainly, if he was going to do something he would have to act soon. The Easter Holidays were only a week away. They broke up on the Thursday. April the fourth...

Suddenly, Danny's face broke into a grin. "And if Thursday is the fourth," he panted. "Then Monday must be the first. April Fool's Day!" He sighed happily. "Perfect!"

And as he continued round the field, he thought of all the tricks he could play on Mr Carlton to make him look really stupid. He could superglue him to a chair. Or a door-handle. Or he could remove the screws from his desk. Or put salt in his tea. Or sugar in his petrol tank. Or slugs in his sandwiches. Or dog-mess in his shoes...

Hot, tired and soaked to the skin, Danny might have been, but by the time he made it back to the changing rooms at last, he was feeling better than he had all day. All week. All term!

It didn't last.

The moment he walked inside, a heavy silence fell. Danny knew that something was wrong.

"What's the matter?" he said to Gary.

Gary turned away, unable to look his friend in the eyes. "I... I'm sorry, mate," he said. "I did try."

"He did," Craig agreed.

"But I'm not in goal," said Danny. "Oh, well, I..." He paused. Something told him that there was worse to come. "Gary?" he said. "What *is* it?" His head began to prickle. "He's gone and done it, hasn't he? He's dropped me from the team."

"Just for the next match," Gary said quickly. "I... I did try," he said for a second time. "Honest, I did..."

"We need you in goal," said Luke Edwards. "None of us wanted it to happen."

"None of us," Maurice Meacham agreed.

"Yeah, I know," said Danny. "I'm not blaming any of you."

He turned and pointed at the closed door to the teacher's changing area. "It's him," he said, his eyes burning with rage.

"Shhh!" Gary hissed. "He might hear you."

Danny turned. "So?" he said. "What else can he do?"

At that moment, the door opened and Mr Carlton himself appeared. He looked Danny up and down.

"That took you long enough," he said. He looked round at the others.

"Unfit, on top of everything else," he commented, and smirked. He turned back to Danny. "Get showered," he said. "And be quick about it. I want to lock up."

Danny nodded. He said nothing, but his head was spinning – with sugar and salt, with superglue and slugs...

With revenge!

Chapter 4

The following day was a Saturday. Danny got up bright and early, dressed quickly and went down for breakfast, taking care to miss the creaking third stair from the top. He didn't want to wake his mum and dad. He couldn't bear their obvious concern about him.

"Are you all right?" they would keep asking. "Is something the matter at school? Do you want to talk about it?" Question after question, until he felt like screaming.

After two Shredded Wheat and a banana, he wrote them a quick note and set off for the rec. The previous evening, he'd told his two friends that he had something planned. Something they needed to discuss. And Gary and Craig had agreed to meet him up the rec at half-past eight.

As he slipped out of the back door, Danny discovered that spring had arrived at long last. It was a warm, breezy morning and the sun was already warm on his back as he trotted along the pavement.

"Hiya," he heard Gary calling, as he went in through the park gates.

"Hiya," said Danny. "Where's Craig?"

"Right behind you," Craig puffed. "I've been trying to catch you up."

Gary laughed. "Unfit, on top of everything else," he said, mimicking Mr Carlton's gruff, nasal voice.

Danny scowled.

"Come on then," said Craig. "You

said you had something important to tell us."

"Yeah," said Gary. "What is it?"

Danny took a deep breath. "I've made a decision," he said, and flicked his hair back from his eyes. "I'm going to get my own back on Mr Carlton." Gary and Craig nodded but remained silent, waiting for the details. "It's April Fool's day on Monday," he said. "And I'm going to play a trick on him. The best trick ever. Make him look really stupid..."

"Brilliant idea," said Craig enthusiastically.

"And he won't dare moan about it," Danny went on. "That'd just make him look even more of a fool."

"I wouldn't bank on it," said Craig. He frowned. "No, I reckon you've got to do something that's so humiliating that he'll want to keep it quiet."

Danny nodded thoughtfully.

"So what *are* you going to do?" said Gary.

Danny frowned. "That's just it," he said. "I can't decide."

"You must have thought of something," Gary persisted.

"Oh, I have," he said. "Loads of things." And he went on to tell them about the superglue on the seat, the salt in the tea, the slugs in the sandwiches...

Gary and Craig were soon rolling about with laughter.

"Slugs!" Gary spluttered. "Can you imagine his face!"

"I could take a photo of him!" said Craig. "Slugman, captured for ever. We could have loads of copies made. Pin them all over the school."

"Or video him!" said Gary. "I could borrow me mum's camcorder."

"Yeah!" said Craig. "And then we could stick it in the video machine in the office. Broadcast it to every class in the school."

"Or send it to *You've Been Framed!*" said Gary, and the pair of them began laughing all over again.

Danny frowned. "I don't know," he said, uncertainly.

Gary and Craig turned towards him in surprise.

"What?" said Craig. "It's a fantastic idea."

"I'm still not sure..."

"Oh, come on Danny," said Gary. "Surely you're not having second thoughts.

"Course not," said Danny, and shook his head. "It's just that – well, *slugs*... You might not actually *see* them. If we are going to use a camcorder, then it's got to be something that everyone can understand without being told."

Gary nodded. "You've got a point."

He paused. "How about the superglue, then? On his chair... What do you think, Craig?"

"I think we can do better than that," said Craig.

Gary sniggered. "We could put it on the toilet seat," he suggested.

"Great idea!" Craig laughed. "But how would you video it?"

"True," said Gary. "Oh, I don't know. What about the bucket of water above the door trick?"

"Pfff!" Danny muttered. "I've tried that before. It never works properly... Though I like the idea of getting him wet." he grinned. "How about if...?

Both Gary and Craig loved Danny's idea. Although harmless, the trick would prove extremely embarrassing for Mr Carlton. And if they managed to capture it all on film as Gary had suggested, it was something they would be able to laugh about again and again and again – *and* show to the rest of the world!

"And you're sure you don't mind helping me?" Danny asked the others.

"Course we don't," said Gary. "It'll be a laugh. Anyway, he can hardly stop the whole team playing, can he?"

Danny shrugged. He wouldn't put anything past Mr Carlton. Certainly it would scupper his own chances of ever getting back into the team – but then Danny considered it a sacrifice worth making. Anything, just so that the horrible man would understand what it was like having everyone laughing at you.

"There's just one thing," said Craig. "We ought to let the others in the class know what's going on. Just so none of them mess it up."

"Yeah, I'd already thought of that," said Gary. "I'm going to tell the whole class what we've got planned on Monday morning – before the register."

Danny nodded. "But what happens if one of them doesn't want to do it – if they warn Mr Carlton."

"No one will," Craig assured him. "Everyone hates him."

Gary picked up the football and kicked it over towards the nearest goal. "Come on," he said. "Seeing as we're here, let's play three 'n in."

Chapter 5

For Danny, Monday's PE lesson went well. Now that Mr Carlton had already dropped him from Wednesday's match against Mickelham Mill, he didn't seem to feel the need to pick on the boy so much. It was only when, at the very end of the lesson, Danny performed a perfect landing off the vaulting box that he spoke to him at all.

"Nice one, Thompson." He smiled unpleasantly. "If only you were as good at football as you are at gymnastics." He swung round and blew his whistle. "Right, you lot," he said. "Go and get showered and changed."

Danny turned away. Mr Carlton would soon be smiling on the other side of his face. Very soon.

Inside the boys' changing room, the atmosphere was electric. Everyone was talking at once in hushed, excited voices about what was about to happen. Craig looked at his watch.

"It's quarter to twelve," he said. "If we're going to do this, we'd better be quick. Otherwise the joke will be on us."

For once, they all got themselves showered double quick, and were towelling themselves down when Danny returned hurriedly to the gym.

"Sir, sir," he said. "It's Gary..."

"Connell?" said Mr Carlton. "What's the matter with him?"

"He's on the floor, sir," Danny said breathlessly. "We think he's fainted."

Mr Carlton abandoned the vaulting box he was wheeling into the storeroom, and followed Danny back to the changing rooms. There was giggling coming from the girls' room. Tracy was peeking out through a crack in the door. As Danny and Mr Carlton went passed, she signalled to the others. It was time to head for the boys' changing room.

"Where is he?" Mr Carlton demanded as he burst in.

"In the showers," came the reply.

"Round the corner, right at the back," said Craig.

Without a moment's hesitation, Mr Carlton dashed inside.

The design of the shower room was key to the boys' plan. Unlike the Junior School, where the showers had been open, the Senior School showers were closed in. Basically, the room was U-shaped. The entrance led into a long, tiled corridor with the main wall on the right, the central wall on the left, and shower-heads sticking out from both sides. Then, at the end of the central wall, the room doubled back on itself, and continued to a dead-end. It meant that if you were in the back of the showers, you could not be seen from the changing room. It was this fact that made the boys' plan possible.

Mr Carlton disappeared from view. "Where? Where is he?" the boys heard him calling. "I can't..."

Danny stepped forwards. A smile tugged at the corners of his mouth. Now he'd show Mr Carlton what it felt like to be made to look stupid the whole time. He reached forwards, grasped the central cold tap and, jaw grimly set, turned it full on.

The shower heads hissed into action. It was all the boys and girls could do to stifle their laughter. Craig took up position with his camera. Gary – hidden away behind a rack of coats between the lockers – pressed the *record* button of the camcorder. They were all set.

From deep inside the shower came a cry of shock and disbelief – like the howl of a wounded animal. The next instant it turned to a roar of anger. "How dare you!" Mr Carlton bellowed and, as he stamped and splashed his way back to the entrance, muttering ominously under his breath, several of the children wondered nervously whether they had gone too far.

Quivering with fury, Mr Carlton burst into the changing room. His time in the showers – though brief – had been enough to soak him. His hair was plastered to his head. The clothes he'd changed into were soaked right through. He looked like a drowned rat!

He glared round at the sea of faces –
boys and girls. Grinning. Laughing.

"April Fool!" they shouted out in
unison, and a dazzling light flashed.

The colour drained from Mr
Carlton's glistening face. With water
streaming down from his clothes to the
floor, he squelched forwards, seized
the camera from Craig's hand and tore
the film from the back.

"Who is responsible for this?" he
demanded.

Silence fell. You could have heard a
pin drop. The pool of water around his
feet grew larger.

"WHO?" he bellowed. "Whose idea
was this?" He turned to Maurice
Meacham. "Do you know?"

"I... It was..." He glanced nervously
over towards the lockers.

"It was everyone's idea," said Craig.
"You know, for April Fool's. We didn't
mean any harm."

Mr Carlton swept his dripping fringe across his forehead. His eyes narrowed and a vein at his temple throbbed menacingly. "Everyone's idea," he said icily. "You don't fool me." He spun round and stormed across the room to Danny.

"What's the betting that tap's got your fingerprints on it, Thompson? You little..."

Danny swallowed nervously. He'd never seen anyone looking so angry. He stepped back and raised his hands defensively.

"Trying to hit me now, are you?" Mr Carlton roared. And with that, he stepped forwards and punched Danny hard in the face.

A gasp echoed round the room. Danny groaned and fell heavily to the floor.

"Self-defence," said Mr Carlton. "You all saw what happened." He swaggered back to the door. "Get to lunch, the lot of you," he said. "Except you, Thompson. You're to stay. I'll deal with you when I've changed."

With Mr Carlton gone, Craig and Maurice helped Danny to his feet and sat him down on the bench. Their brief moment of triumph had turn horribly sour, leaving them all shaky, edgy.

"Are you all right, mate?" said Craig.

Danny nodded blankly. "I suppose so," he said and fingered the top of his cheek delicately. "Shwooo!" he said and winced. "It hurts."

"He's going to get done for that," said Craig angrily. "Teachers aren't allowed to go around hitting pupils."

"Does it show?" asked Danny.

Craig nodded. "You might even get a black eye," he said. "You've got to report him, Danny. He can't be allowed to get away with it."

"He'll twist everything round, of course," said Maurice. "Then it'll be our word against his..."

"Oh no it won't," came a voice from behind him.

Maurice spun round to see Gary emerging from behind the row of coats and jackets hanging between the lockers. He was clutching the camcorder.

"Did you get it all?" said Craig.

"Every last second," Gary said.

"Fantastic!" said Craig. "Come on, then. Let's go. We'll show it to Mrs Merson – she'll know what to do. Danny?"

"But I can't," said Danny. "He told me to stay here."

"Stay here!" Gary exclaimed. "With that maniac? You must be out of your tiny mind!"

"And if you come with us," said Craig, "Mrs Merson will be able to see just how hard he hit you."

Danny nodded uncertainly. "Yeah, but," he said, "what if it just gets everyone into trouble for joining in the trick in the first place?"

"What he did was wrong," said Craig firmly. "Very wrong. And we're going to nail him for it."

"Yeah, but..." Danny began again.

"Oh, blimey!" said Gary. "Look mate, we're going to show it to her anyway. She's got to know what kind of a teacher Mr Carlton is. So are you coming with us, or not?" He glanced round nervously. "He's going to be back any minute, so you'd better make up your mind pretty quick."

"OK," said Danny finally. He leapt to his feet and grabbed his bag. "I'll come with you. Let's go."

Chapter 6

"Enter," came Mrs Merson's strident voice in response to Craig's timid knock on the head-teacher's door.

Gary turned the handle, and the three boys went inside. The first thing they noticed was that she wasn't alone. A heavy-set, grey-haired man was seated in the chair in front of her desk. Mrs Merson looked up. "Aah, Gary, Craig and Danny, isn't it?" she said.

They nodded.

"As you can see," Mrs Merson went on, "I'm in the middle of a meeting at the moment. Could this wait until later, please?"

Danny and Craig went to leave, but Gary remained where he was. "I... I don't think it can, Mrs Merson," he said. "It's really important. A matter of life and death," he added dramatically.

Mrs Merson sighed and climbed to her feet. "I'm sorry about this, Mr Trill," she said. She turned to the boys. "Mr Trill is the head governor," she said. "A very important man. I..." She paused and peered into Danny's face. "Have you been *fighting*, Danny?" she asked.

"No, Mrs Merson... That is... Yes... I..." Danny blustered.

"That's why we're here," Gary said, coming to his friend's aid. "Danny got hit."

"And hit hard, by the look of it," said Mrs Merson sternly. She turned to Mr Trill. "As you know," she said, "we take a very dim view of bullying at St Botolph's and I do like to get to the bottom of any incident as soon as possible."

"Of course," said Mr Trill. "You go ahead."

"Thank you," said Mrs Merson. She turned her attention back to Danny. "So, who did this to you?"

Gary stepped forwards and held out the camcorder. "It's all on here," he said.

Mrs Merson's eyes narrowed. "You recorded it?" she said suspiciously, "But—"

"Please, Mrs Merson," Gary said, and swallowed nervously. "Just watch it. Then you'll understand..."

"Oh, very well, then," she said and her face broke into a smile. "But if this is some kind of an April Fool prank, I'm afraid you're too late. It's gone twelve."

"Just look," Gary said. He pressed *play* and handed the camcorder to Mrs Merson, who peered down into the viewfinder.

As she watched, the three boys knew exactly what she must be looking at from the changing expressions which passed across her face. Eyebrow raised puzzlement at first as Mr Carlton headed into the shower. Then purse-lipped reproach – with perhaps just a hint of amusement – as Danny turned the shower on.

"*This* was the April Fool's prank, I take it, Danny," she said without looking up.

"Yes, Mrs Merson," said Danny sheepishly. "It—"

Suddenly, Mrs Merson gasped – and the boys knew that she had seen the blow itself.

"Oh, my goodness!" she exclaimed.

Visibly shaken, she placed the

camcorder on to the table and scratched her forehead thoughtfully. The three boys looked at each other. What was she going to say? What would she do? Finally, she looked up.

"Why did you record it, Gary?" she asked.

Gary shuffled about awkwardly. "We thought it would be ... a laugh," he said.

"A laugh," Mrs Merson repeated flatly. "And you planned to show others in the school what happened, I take it."

Gary nodded. "And I'm sorry, Mrs Merson. It was a stupid idea."

"But ... but it's been going on for ages," Craig butted in. "Mr Carlton's always picking on Danny. The whole time – ever since we started in the Seniors. And it's not fair! That's why we decided to play a trick on him in the first place."

Mrs Merson took a sharp intake of breath. "Danny," she said. "In all my years of teaching, I—"

Before she could say another word, the door abruptly burst open. It was Mr Carlton – back in his tracksuit. "Mrs Merson," he said angrily. "I wish to make a formal complaint about..."

He paused. The room was not as empty as he had expected. He looked at the head governor. He looked at Gary, at Craig – at Danny.

"Thompson!" he bellowed. "I thought I told you to wait for me in the changing rooms." He turned back to Mrs Merson. "First he humiliates me—"

"Mr Carlton," said Mrs Merson. "You will not—"

"Then he raises his fists to me – *and* I've got witnesses—"

"Mr *Carlton*," said Mrs Merson more sharply.

"And now he has deliberately disobeyed my instructions to—"

"*Mr* Carlton!" Mrs Merson shouted. "*Will* you be quiet!"

Stunned into silence, Mr Carlton was left opening and shutting his mouth like a goldfish.

Mrs Merson tapped the camcorder. "I have seen everything that took place," she said. "Everything."

Mr Carlton squirmed uncomfortably. "Yes, well, in that case you'll know—"

"I know this," Mrs Merson interrupted. "That in thirty-five years of teaching, I have never before witnessed anything so barbaric."

"But I ... he ... they..." Mr Carlton blustered.

"I am well aware of all the circumstances," Mrs Merson continued. "But your behaviour was absolutely unacceptable. Do you understand me? Un-ac-cept-able! You are suspended forthwith! Please collect your belongings and leave the school at once."

Mr Carlton's eyes narrowed. "You can't suspend me. I..."

"I most certainly can!" stormed Mrs Merson, "as I'm sure Mr Trill would be only too happy to confirm."

Mr Trill nodded seriously.

"And you may be sure that if I have any say in the matter," Mrs Merson continued. "Then you will never teach again. Now go."

As Mr Carlton finally left the room, slamming the door behind him, Danny – who had been staring at his feet the whole time – looked up. His eyes had turned watery. His shoulders were shaking. Having been so brave for so long, he could no longer hide how much the entire situation had upset him.

"It's all right, Danny, mate," said

Gary, squeezing him awkwardly round the shoulder.

"It's all over, now," Craig added.

"I ... I know," Danny sobbed. "It's just such a relief." He sniffed and wiped his eyes. "Look at me," he said, smiling weakly. "I can't stop shaking."

"Shock," said Mr Trill. "He needs a nice cup of sweet tea."

Mrs Merson nodded. "Or would you prefer a cold drink?" she asked Danny.

"Yes please," he said.

Mrs Merson buzzed through to the school secretary, and placed an order for three bottles of orangeade. Then, stepping round to the front of the desk, she spoke to the three boys.

"Whilst I cannot condone the trick you played," she said slowly, deliberately, "I can understand how and why it came about." She frowned. "Such behaviour, of course, must never be repeated."

"No, Mrs Merson," the three of them chorused.

"However..." She breathed in sharply. "Craig, your camera film got ruined," she said. "When you buy a new one, bring the receipt to me. The school will pay."

"Thanks, Mrs Merson," said Craig gratefully.

"And Gary," she said, as she reached round for the camcorder and handed it to him. "You may take this, but I'd be grateful if you could let me keep the video – at least for the time being."

"That's fine," said Gary. He pressed the eject button and gave her the video cassette.

"Thank you. Now, if the pair of you could wait outside, I'd like a private word with Danny. Take a seat, Danny," she said.

"Would you like me to leave, too?" asked Mr Trill.

"No," said Mrs Merson thoughtfully. "No, please stay."

As the two boys were leaving, Mrs Merson's secretary arrived with the orangeade. Gary and Craig took their bottles outside.

Danny sat back down in the chair and unscrewed the bottle-top. It hissed and fizzed. He leant his head back, poured the sweet, bubbling liquid into his mouth, swirled it round and swallowed.

As if by magic, Danny felt instantly calmer. The shaking stopped. He drank some more, and looked up.

"Feel any better?" said Mrs Merson.

"Much," said Danny.

"And your cheek?" she said.

"It still throbs," said Danny. "But it's not too bad..."

Mrs Merson's face clouded with concern. She shook her head slowly. "Danny," she said. "I owe you an apology."

She glanced over at Mr Trill, who was nodding solemnly.

"Your first experience of St Botolph's has clearly been a dreadful one. And it is a situation for which I take full responsibility."

"It was just... I mean..."

"As you may or may not be aware, your parents have been in to see me twice this year."

Danny's jaw dropped open. This was news to him.

"They were concerned about your work – about your general attitude. They said you'd changed..."

Danny hung his head. It was true. Not only had his marks been getting worse and worse all year, but he seemed to spend his whole time at home arguing.

"I told them not to worry," Mrs Merson went on. "I said it was teething troubles – what with being at a new school and everything." She sighed. "Will either of your parents be at home now?"

"Mum should be," said Danny. "She only works mornings."

"Then I'll call her," Mrs Merson said. "I'll explain what's been happening."

Danny nodded uncertainly. Mrs Merson leant forwards and patted him on the knees.

"A fresh start," she said. "That's what we need. A new beginning. I can't undo what's already been done but I can make sure that, from now on, things are going to change."

Danny frowned. After everything that had happened, it all sounded too easy.

"And don't worry," she said. "Leave everything to me. You're going to be just fine."

Chapter 7

Mrs Merson was as good as her word. Things did change. That evening, his parents couldn't have been nicer to him – and the following morning...!

Word of the fight between Mr Carlton and Danny Thompson had spread round the school like wildfire. And when Danny came through the school gates – his black eye shining just as Craig had thought it would – he was immediately surrounded by a large group of admirers, from the girls and boys in his own class to kids from years ten, eleven and twelve who had themselves been bullied over the years by Mr Carlton.

"Well done!" they all said. And, "He had it coming." And, "Someone should have done something about him years ago."

Then, before he knew what was happening, Danny found himself being hoisted up into the air on top of a mass of shoulders, and paraded around the playground – the hero of the hour, wearing the scars of battle with pride. Round and round, they went; faster and faster. Shouting. Laughing. If the bell hadn't gone for the start of school, they might have kept on all morning.

"OK. Sit down all of you," said Miss MacPherson their form-teacher as 7M burst noisily into the classroom. "And that includes you, Luke." She paused. "Before I take the register, I've got an important message from Mr Berryman."

Danny's ears pricked up.

"It concerns the football team," she continued. "Mr Berryman has taken over as coach and—"

A cheer went up, drowning Miss MacPherson out. It was the best possible news they could have had. With a smile playing around her eyes, Miss MacPherson waited for everyone to quieten down before continuing.

"*And*," she repeated finally, "since yesterday's session had to be cancelled, there will be a special session after school this afternoon at three-thirty to prepare for tomorrow's match. Anyone without their kit will be allowed to fetch it at lunch-time." She looked up. "Any questions?"

Gary put his hand up. "Only one," he said. "Do you think we're going to beat Mickelham tomorrow?"

Miss MacPherson raised an eyebrow. "Is it an important game?" she asked.

"Crucial, Miss," Gary assured her.

She smiled. "Then I'm sure you will," she said.

"OK, listen up, lads," said Mr Berryman. "The situation is close. Really close. After last Wednesday's draw, we've ended up level peggings with Mickelham Mill at the top of the group. Both teams have won three, drawn two and lost one, and the goal aggregate is twelve apiece, which means – as I'm sure you're only too aware – we've got to beat our old rivals to earn a place in the final."

Gary nodded earnestly. "We've beaten them before, sir," he said. "We can do it again."

"That's the spirit, Gary," said Mr Berryman. "And after the excellent work on the field that you've shown me this afternoon, I have absolute confidence that you will win."

The boys beamed proudly.

"Do you really mean that?" said Craig.

Mr Berryman laughed. "With the skill you showed at heading and passing and tackling, are you joking? Play that well tomorrow, and you could beat Brazil!" He paused. "There's just one thing…"

The boys looked up, wondering what he was about to say next.

"This 3–5–2 formation you're playing in." He winced. "I don't know…"

"It wasn't our idea," said Maurice hurriedly. "We always used to play 4–4–2 before Mr—"

"Yes," Mr Berryman broke in thoughtfully. "Standard. Solid…"

"I reckon we want something more attacking, though," said Craig. "4–2–4, maybe."

"My thoughts exactly," said Mr Berryman. "We need to really go for it. After all, there's everything to play for.

And as my old football coach used to say to me, victory is not for the faint-hearted."

Once again, the boys' hearts swelled – with pride and anticipation. Each and every one of them could picture himself stepping up to receive the cup. For the third time. For the hat-trick. Just one match away.

"Right then," said Mr Berryman. "I think that's about all I want to say. Get a good night's sleep tonight. And good luck for tomorrow." He winked. "Not that I think you need it!"

A cheer went up. Mr Berryman climbed to his feet. The pep-talk was at an end.

One matter, however, had *not* been raised. Gary had forgotten all about it, while Danny was far too embarrassed to bring it up. In the end, it was Ricky Baker who spoke.

"Sir?" he said.

Mr Berryman looked round. "Yes, Ricky."

"Sir, now that Danny's back in the team, there's something I wanted to ask."

"Ask away."

Ricky took a deep breath. The others listened. "Can me and Danny swap positions? He's a better goalie than me and I really like playing in defence and..."

Mr Berryman burst out laughing. "Why the worried face?" he said. "Of course you can. So long as Danny's happy with that."

He looked round. Danny stepped forwards, a huge grin stretching from ear to ear. "Yes, sir, I am," he said. "Very very happy!"

Chapter 8

At three-thirty on the dot, the whistle blew to start the match between St Botolph's and Mickelham Mill. The reds versus the greens. A re-run of the previous year's final.

At first, the game was fast and furious – enthusiastic rather than accurate, with too many passes going astray on both sides. Time and again, a clever build up was ruined at the last minute by a sloppy error. It was only after Gary had got everyone to calm things down a little that matters began to improve.

Having saved a weak shot at goal, Danny took his time before passing the ball out. Only when he was sure everyone was in position did he roll the ball to Ricky Baker. Ricky nudged the ball forwards a little, tempting their number seven forward. Then, when he moved, Ricky tapped the ball over to Maurice, who took it up the line before crossing it to Luke.

The pass was perfect. It flew down through the air and landed just in front of him. What was more, Gary, who was steaming up the field, was still onside. Without a moment's hesitation, Luke stepped forwards and took the ball on the volley.

It scudded across the grass, past their number eight and on towards Gary.

A cry went round the crowd. "St Botolph's! St Botolph's!" Although they were playing away, there were as many St Botolph's as Mickelham Mill supporters – and they were far louder!

Out of the corner of his eye, Gary could see their number three hurtling towards him. The ball got closer. So did the defender.

"Stay cool!" Gary told himself.

At the other end of the pitch, Danny was telling himself the same thing. "Just stay cool," he muttered. "Keep your head. You're doing fine."

Being back in goal after such a long time was proving more nerve-wracking than he'd imagined. He found he needed to concentrate hard on all the little things that used to be completely automatic. Judging the speed of incoming balls. Timing his leaps. Placing his kicks. But it *was* coming back. Slowly but surely, he was growing in confidence.

The score was 0–0. He hadn't let any in. And, as Gary continued his run to the descending ball, Danny's heart raced. This could be it. This could be the attack which put them one goal up.

"Go on, Gary!" he bellowed. "You can do it!"

The ball drew level, just as the defender arrived. Gary dummied to the left, then flicked the ball deftly to the right. The number three was left hopelessly off-balance. Seizing the advantage, Gary suddenly accelerated and drove the ball at the goal.

The goalkeeper never stood a chance. A triumphant roar went up as the ball thudded into the back of the net. Only fifteen minutes into the match and they'd already gone ahead. St Botolph's one, Mickelham Mill nil.

"Yes!" Danny exclaimed, and punched the air.

The battle was on – and St Botolph's sensed victory. Four minutes later, Luke headed a superb corner from Craig to make it 2–0.

"Easy! Easy! Easy!" the St Botolph's supporters roared.

The score was still 2–0 at half-time. Mr Berryman came on to the pitch with a tray of quartered oranges and eleven plastic cups of lemon barley.

"You're doing yourselves proud, lads," he said. "Excellent work. You keep playing like this and you'll not only get through to the final, you'll win it!" He put his hands on his hips and looked round seriously. "But you know what they say, it isn't over till..."

"The final whistle," the boys all shouted back and laughed.

"A cliche, but true nonetheless," said Mr Berryman. "Just keep your heads. And nothing silly. All right?"

The boys nodded.

"Go on then," he said. "Get back out there and give it everything you've got!"

* * *

If anything, the second half of the match started even better than the first. St Botolph's were all over the opposition, launching attack after attack, and defending solidly and skilfully whenever they needed to. Mickelham Mill hardly got a look in.

In the fifty-eighth minute Gary scored his second goal of the match – a clever chip which caught two defenders and the goalie completely by surprise. Ten minutes later, Wesley made it 4–0 with an express-train of a shot which was still rising as it slammed into the top left hand corner of the goal.

Then something happened. Nothing that could affect the outcome of the match, but something that surprised the rest of the team nevertheless. Danny let in a goal. And an easy goal at that. A goal he would have saved ninety-nine times out of a hundred.

Immediately after they'd kicked off

after the fourth goal, the Mickelham Mill number seven had decided to go it alone. He drove determinedly through the St Botolph's midfield and, seeing the heavy defence advancing towards him, had a stab at goal.

Mid-height, mid-speed – it wasn't a great shot. It wasn't even a particularly good shot. All Danny had to do was step to the left to catch it safely. And yet, just as the ball was almost in his hands, he had seemed to falter. To forget what he was doing. The lapse in concentration proved fatal.

Horrified, he watched as the ball struck the side of his hand, and bounced away. He leapt after it, grasping at the air, but it was no good. The ball was already over the line.

After that, the game slowed right down. Gary echoed Mr Berryman's advice that they shouldn't do anything silly.

"We're 4–1 up," he said. "Let's keep it that way."

The last minutes ticked uneventfully away, with St Botolph's using the opportunity to practice their passing skills. The final whistle blew. The team cheered triumphantly. The crowd went wild.

For the third year running, St Botolph's had made it through to the final. The hat-trick was only one match away!

It was only later, when Danny, Gary and Craig were on the coach heading back across town that Gary remembered the one glitch in an otherwise perfect performance. He turned to Danny.

"That goal you let in," he said. "It wasn't like you."

Danny frowned. "I know," he said.

"So what happened?" Gary persisted.

"I got distracted," said Danny. "I... I thought I heard something."

Craig looked round. "What?" he said.

"Nothing," said Danny. He shrugged. "You'll think I'm crazy."

"Come on," said Gary. "Tell us."

"We won't laugh," added Craig.

Danny took a big breath. "It was just before Wesley scored that fourth goal," he said. "Someone in the crowd shouted out – at one of their defenders I guess..."

"What?" said Gary and Craig together.

"*Cinderella*," said Danny, and smiled weakly.

"You don't think Mr Carlton was there, do you?" said Craig. "He wouldn't..."

"Course not," said Danny. "But it was just the word. Hearing it again – it brought back so many horrible memories."

Craig nodded seriously. "I can understand that," he said.

"Me, too," said Gary. "But it's over now, Danny. It really is. Mr Carlton's gone and we're through to the final. You can't afford to get distracted like that."

"Oh, come on," Craig protested. "You're being a bit hard on him."

"No," said Danny. "Gary's right. If we're going to win the hat-trick we've got to play like we've never played before. And do you know what?"

"What?"

"We *are* going to win!"

Chapter 9

There had been a lot of controversy about the suggestion to hold the final on the first Saturday of the holiday. "It'll be a disaster," some said. "No one will turn up," others maintained.

But when it came to a vote, the decision was carried easily. Just as in the previous year, when the board had agreed to allow local sponsorship of the teams, so this year the date and venue for the Mereside Borough Junior Cup were to change.

The reason was simple. There was to be a huge Easter Fair at the town

Sports Centre on the Saturday. The money raised would go towards building a new children's ward at the local hospital. The organizers thought that if they combined the two events – the fair and the cup final – then the takings would be higher than ever.

And so it was that at half-past one on Saturday, April the sixth, St Botolph's, playing in the red strip of their sponsors, *Pringle's Paints* and Milton Comp, in their *Aquatic Supplies* blue, trotted out on to the field to the rousing cheers of the biggest crowd of spectators the final had ever drawn.

"Come on you Paint Boys!" roared the St Botolph's supporters.

"Come on you blues!" responded their opponents.

The two captains walked to the centre of the pitch. The referee tossed the coin.

"Heads," said Gary.

"Heads it is," said the ref.

Gary looked round. It was a bright, cloudless day. At the moment, the sun was high above their heads. By the second half, however, it would have sunk much lower. That was the time to have the sun shining in your opponents' eyes.

"Ends," he announced.

Danny marched up to the far goal, the sun beating down hotly on the back of his head. That morning, he'd had a haircut – short, like he always used to have it. *Not* because Mr Carlton had told him to, but because *he* wanted to. Looking back, he was no longer even that sure why he'd let it grow so long in the first place.

"This is it," he told himself grimly. "The final." He breathed in deeply. "We can do it!" He breathed in again. "We can win." And again. "For the third time. The hat-trick. We're gonna win that cup – for ever!"

The match started slowly. Much more slowly than against Mickelham Mill. There was too much at stake. The teams were evenly matched and whoever took the lead was likely to keep it. Milton were playing in standard 4–4–2 positions. St Botolph's were in the more aggressive 4–2–4 formation which had served them so well in their previous match. The whole team was hoping that it would do the trick for a second time.

After a finely balanced first half-hour – with both teams testing, teasing and probing their opponents – Gary decided to speed things up a bit. After all, the last thing any of them wanted was for the match to be decided on a penalty shoot-out.

Seizing the ball from Craig's feet, he raced up the left wing, past their number ten, their number eight, their number four. At the other side of the pitch, Luke had seen what was going on. He sprinted into the middle of the field and, taking care to keep a couple of defenders between him and the goal, inched his way on towards the box. Wesley and Craig moved up behind him.

Gary's cross, when it came, was a gem. It landed just in front of Luke, who raced forwards and struck the ball hard with his left foot.

"Yeah!" screamed the St Botolph's supporters. At last, their patience had been rewarded.

But no! It wasn't a goal. The ball had struck the crossbar and bounced back into play. The crowd groaned. Wesley and Craig and Luke raced forwards to finish it off, but their number two got there first. Keeping his head, he chipped it deftly past Wesley and punted it up the pitch.

St Botolph's were in instant disarray. Expecting to score, they had dropped their guard and were all far too far forward. Now they were under attack, and there was no one there to defend.

Sprinting across towards the goal, Ricky attempted to cut off their advancing number seven. Inside the penalty box the pair of them went. Then, with his arms spread-eagled and his right leg stretched out in front of him, Ricky launched forwards into a desperate sliding tackle. It was dangerous. If he made contact with the ball, he would save a goal. If he struck the player, however, he would give one away in the form of a penalty. In the event he missed both!

With a sudden change of speed, the number seven slowed down, brought the ball round on to his left foot, and kicked it with the inside of his boot.

Danny chewed his bottom lip. "Come on," he urged himself. "You can do it."

He dived. The crowd fell still. Curling viciously, the ball grazed Danny's outstretched fingers and hurtled into the corner of the net.

There was nothing he could have done – not that that made things any better. St Botolph's were 1–0 down. It was going to be an uphill struggle from now on and, despite several superb attempts on the opposition goal, the score was still 1–0 at half-time.

Mr Berryman was the first on the pitch with cartons of juice and words of advice.

"You're doing fine, lads," he said encouragingly. "And Danny," he said. "I don't want you to think about that goal for a second. There isn't a goalie on this earth who could have saved it. You're having a fantastic game," he grinned. "Keep it up. And the rest of you," he said, looking round the circle of eager faces. "Just keep putting the pressure on the way you're doing, and we'll get 'em for sure in the second half."

He told them to play to their opponents' weaker side. He told them to watch out for the number eight. He told them, above all, to enjoy themselves.

Gary rubbed his sweaty forehead on his sleeve and grinned. "Oh, we intend to," he said. "Got the sun in their eyes now, haven't they? Come on, lads," he announced. "Let's dazzle them!"

The moment the second-half kicked off, the St Botolph's supporters sensed a difference in their team's attitude. Passes became crisper. Headers, more accurate. And every time someone from Milton kicked the ball over the line, St Botolph's took the throw-in before the opposition had time to re-group properly.

"Keep your shape!" Mr Berryman bellowed from the sideline.

And they did. The attackers attacked, time after time, with balls pumped out to them from midfield, while the defenders closed down every single attempt at goal with ruthless efficiency.

With thirty minutes left to play, it was clear which side was on top. Everyone – both on and off the pitch – knew that it was only a matter of time before St Botolph's equalized. And in the sixty-eighth minute, that was precisely what they did.

Gary had taken a running-shot from just outside the penalty area. The ball had passed between two defenders who, unluckily for their goalie, were unsighting him. When he saw the ball suddenly speeding towards him from the glare of the low sun, he leaped across the goal in a frantic bid to stop it.

At first, as the ball hammered against his gloves, it looked as though he'd been successful. But then – to his and all the Milton supporters' horror – it bounced back away from him. Gary, who still hadn't stopped his run, was there at once to capitalize on his mistake. He trapped the ball at his feet, drew back his right leg and booted it squarely into the back of the net.

The crowd bellowed their approval and a chant of "Paint Boys, Paint Boys, Oi! Oi! Oi!" went up.

With the equalizing goal finally under their belts, St Botolph's raised their game another notch. They won a free kick from a dirty foul just beyond the halfway line. Maurice took it quickly, chipping the ball over to his left. Craig gathered the ball and swept back towards the middle. Their number eight was in front of him. Luke was to his right.

He kicked it firmly to Luke and kept running. The ball bounced off Luke's extended right foot and back. Craig picked it up again and continued his run.

"Over here!" Gary yelled from his left.

Maybe the Milton players thought that their captain was the only striker they had. Whatever, when he called, two of their defenders moved towards him. A hole opened up. Craig ran into it, flicked the ball on to his right foot and booted it hard. 2–1! At last they had gone ahead.

"YEAH!" Craig cried out and skidded across the grass on his knees, fists clenched and head raised to the sky.

All round the pitch, the spectators

went crazy. A sea of red scarves pitched and tossed as every St Botolph's supporter leapt about with their arms waving above their heads. While on the pitch itself, Craig was surrounded by the rest of the team, all slapping him on the back and telling him how brilliant he was.

"Come on then," said Gary. "Ten minutes to go and the cup's ours."

Ten minutes in football, however, is a long time. With less than three minutes to go, the Milton number eight made a sudden dash for goal. He was fast, but Ricky was there to close him down till support came. But the number eight wasn't about to wait. He kicked the ball – slap – against Ricky's hand.

"Handball!" the Mickelham Mill players appealed.

"No way!" Gary yelled. "It was ball to hand. Not hand to ball."

"Handball! Handball!" the chant went round the crowd.

The referee looked to his assistant. The linesman's flag went up. The referee blew his whistle.

"NO!" screamed Gary. "Are you deaf, blind or what? It was ball to hand. He did it deliberately!"

The referee turned on him furiously. "One more word out of you, and you're off!"

"Calm down, Gary," said Craig, and led his friend away. "It's a penalty. Just pray they don't score."

In the goal, Danny was trying to compose himself. A penalty! Just when it was looking as though the match was in the bag. He rubbed his gloved hands together and watched their number eight placing the ball.

The sun burnt into the back of his neck. Thank heavens Gary had chosen ends so cleverly, he thought. With the sun in his eyes, he'd never have stood a chance. The number eight stepped backwards. Danny swallowed. If he could save this one penalty, he would save himself the misery of another five in the shoot-out.

"You can do it!" he told himself. "You must do it!"

Suddenly the Milton striker was running forwards. Danny committed himself. The ball was kicked. Danny leaped to his left. And the ball flew – to the left as well. Danny was still in mid-air when the ball thudded against his chest. He hugged it towards him and tumbled down to the ground.

He *had* done it!

A moment later, the referee blew the final whistle. The crowd roared with triumph and jubilation. St Botolph's had achieved what no other team had ever achieved before. They'd won the

Mereside Borough Junior Cup for three years in succession. Now it was theirs to keep.

A chant went up. A chant that echoed round and round the pitch; a chant so loud that even those at the Easter fair who had no interest in football came over to see what was going on. Something wonderful had happened. Something unique in the history of the Mereside Borough Junior Cup.

"Hat-trick!" The words rang out. "Hat-trick! Hat-trick! Hat-trick!"

COMING SOON

FOOTBALL MAD 4

TEAMWORK

Year assembly was generally not the kid's favourite part of the day, but that particular morning, Mrs Merson their head-teacher, had something important to say. Something which caught the imagination of all the girls and boys in year seven.

"I want to begin by congratulating all of you who played any part in the Easter Fair," she said. "Particularly the under-twelve football team – the erm... *Paint Boys*."

A ripple of approval went round. Gary, Danny and Craig exchanged proud glances.

"As I'm sure you all know, St Botolph's beat Milton, 2–1, in the final of the Mereside Borough Junior Cup."

A cheer resounded round the hall.

"What you may not know," Mrs Merson continued, "is that the crowds drawn to the match resulted in the Easter Fair itself being a tremendous success. This year, the takings were way up on all previous years. In fact, I am pleased to announce that, taking everything into account, the amount raised was a staggering..."

A hush fell. You could have heard a pin drop. The money was all to go towards the New Children's Ward Fund at the local hospital. And since every single child knew someone – a brother or sister or a friend – who'd had to go to the *old* children's ward, they all understood how important it was to raise the money quickly.

So just how much *had* the Easter Fair raised?

Mrs Merson was still teasing them.

"...A remarkable. An almost un-believable..." She paused. "£23,419.27p!"

There was a gasp, followed by a moment of silence, and then a deafening roar went up which echoed round and round the hall. Of course, everyone knew that some important sponsors had guaranteed large donations – but twenty-three thousand pounds! It hardly seemed possible.

Mrs Merson waited for the clapping and cheering to subside before continuing.

"The money will all go to the hospital fund," she said. "And very grateful they are. However..." She paused. The children waited for her to continue with bated breath. "Despite the success of the Easter Fair, there is still a long way to go before we reach the target. So I want you all to put on your thinking-caps and come up with ideas for raising more money. Bring-and-buy sales. Sponsored walks. Raffles. Christmas cards..."

"What about a non-uniform day?" Maurice Meacham called out. "Everyone has to pay a pound to wear what they want."

"Excellent idea, Maurice," said Mrs Merson. "I—"

"Or a marathon read-in," suggested Judy Reeves, who was a bit of a swot.

"Or a disco," shouted Toyah Langton, who was not.

"Or school tea-towels," somebody shouted from the back.

"Or printed T-shirts," shouted somebody else.

Mrs Merson raised her hands for quiet. "Anyone who has a good idea should either talk about it with their form-teacher or come to see me," she said and smiled. "And good luck, all of you. I know that all the other schools in the area are making plans of their own. But I have absolute confidence that, if we all work together, then St Botolph's will make the biggest contribution of all."

As the boys and girls filed from the hall and streamed off towards their lessons, an excited buzz filled the corridors. Gary, Danny and Craig had English that first lesson, with Miss MacPherson – who also happend to be their form-teacher. The moment they walked into the classroom, all three of them cornered her.

"Miss, Miss," they chorused.

"We've had a brilliant idea," said Gary.

"For raising money," Danny explained.

"We could—" Craig began.

"Sit down, boys, please," said Miss MacPherson. "When everyone's in their places, we'll discuss your idea."

The whole class scurried quickly to their seats. Miss MacPherson turned to Gary. "Right then," she said. "Tell me about this brilliant idea of yours."

Gary grinned. "A charity football match," he said.

Miss MacPherson raised her eyebrows.

"I don't know," she said. "Sometimes I think the whole world's gone football mad."

"But, Miss," said Craig. "Mrs Merson did say that it was the football that drew the crowds to the Easter Fair. This time, we'll just have the match – but charge all the spectators to watch it."

Miss MacPherson nodded. "And who would you play?" she asked.

Gary looked down. A smile was playing round his mouth. "We thought the teachers," he said.

"You could play in goal, Miss," said Danny.

"Yes, nice idea," said Miss McPherson. "But I think not." Then ignoring the chorus of protests, she went on. "What about one of the other local schools? Or perhaps you could play a fathers' team."

Gary nodded. "We could do," he said, "but..."

"I've got a much better idea," a voice piped up from the back.

Everyone turned round and looked at Tracy Taylor expectantly.

"Well?" said Miss MacPherson.

Tracy grinned. "Simple," she said. "We make it girls versus boys."

For a moment there was silence as the suggestion sunk in. Girls versus boys. It would be a walkover – and who'd want to pay to watch a match that was a foregone conclusion. Then again, the girl's team – although not as successful as the Paint Boys – wasn't bad. They'd made it to the semis of the local Girls Club League. And Tracy herself was a formidably determined captain.

A murmur began to go round the classroom. A murmur that grew louder and louder until everyone was chanting.

"Boys! Boys! Boys!" cried the boys.

"Girls! Girls! Girls!" the girls chanted back.

"Boys!"

"Girls!"

"BOYS"

"GIRLS"

"BOYS!"

"*GIRLS!*"

Miss MacPherson's arm shot up. She wanted quiet and she wanted it now.

"Girls!" called a lone voice. It was Tracy's closest friend, Toyah. She spun round. "Sorry, Miss."

"Hmmph!" said Miss MacPherson. She looked around at the sea of expectant facts. "Well," she said finally, "if there's as much interest for the match *outside* the class as there is *inside*, you could do very well indeed." She turned to Tracy. "And you're sure you want to go ahead with this?"

"Oh, yes," said Tracy. "Aren't we, girls?" she added, looking round at the others in the team.

"And Gary?" said Miss MacPherson.

"You bet!" said Gary.

HURRICANE HAMISH
Mark Jefferson

HURRICANE HAMISH
THE CALYPSO CRICKETER

Hurricane Hamish has always been a bit special – ever since he was found washed up on a Caribbean beach wrapped in an MCC towel. He's only twelve, but he can bowl fast. Really fast. So fast he might be about to play for the West Indies...

HURRICANE HAMISH
THE CRICKET WORLD CUP

Hurricane Hamish is back – and now he's in England, determined to help the West Indies win the Cricket World Cup. But England is so cold! The grounds are so wet and slippery that Hurricane can't even stay standing, let alone bowl fast...

"The ideal literary companion for this summer's Carnival of Cricket – the World Cup."
Lord MacLaurin, Chairman of the England and Wales Cricket Board

"Mark Jefferson has scored a real winner with Hurricane Hamish ... this pacey romp of a book."
Christina Hardyment, The Independent

"A novel which, like its hero, has pace and heart."
Nicolette Jones, The Sunday Times